for Barbara

First American Edition

Published in 1978 by The Viking Press, 625 Madison Avenue, New York, N.Y. 10022
Printed in Great Britain

1 2 3 4 5 82 81 80 79 78

Library of Congress Cataloging in Publication Data
Grimm, Jakob Ludwig Karl, 1785-1863. The twelve dancing princesses.
Retold from the authors' *Die zertanzten Schuhe*.
Summary: A retelling of the tale of twelve
princesses who dance secretly all night long, and the
soldier who follows them and discovers where they dance.
(1. Fairy tales. 2. Folklore – Germany)
I. Grimm, Wilhelm Karl, 1786-1859, joint author.
II. Le Cain, Errol. III. Title.
PZ8.G882Tw 1978 398.2'2 (E) 78 – 8578
ISBN 0–670–73358–x

Illustrated by Errol Le Cain

The Twelve Dancing Princesses

retold from a story by the Brothers Grimm

THE VIKING PRESS
New York

There was once a king who had twelve wonderfully beautiful daughters. They slept together in one great room, in twelve beds all in a row, and every evening the king locked them in. And yet every morning their shoes were worn out, as if they had danced all night.

The princesses would never admit that they had done anything but sleep peacefully in their beds, but the king was determined to find out the truth. He issued a proclamation announcing that anyone who could discover where the princesses danced at night should be allowed to choose one of them for his wife, and inherit the kingdom after the king's death. But he must find the answer within three days.

Very soon a prince arrived at the palace, offering to try to discover the secret. The king made him very welcome and when evening came he was shown to a chamber which opened off the great room where the princesses slept. There a splendid bed was waiting for him, and the door between the rooms was left ajar, so that the princesses could not steal away without his seeing them.

They all greeted him most politely and the eldest brought him a cup of wine. As he drank it, he thought how beautiful she was, and that was the last thought he had until the morning. Then he awoke and saw the princesses sleeping peacefully in their beds, and their worn-out shoes standing in a row. The same thing happened the next night and the night after that, and then the prince was dismissed from the palace, since he had failed in his task.

Many more princes followed him but they were all just as unsuccessful.

One day a poor soldier was limping along the high road that led to the king's palace. He had been wounded in battle and now he would never be able to fight again. On the way he met an old woman, who said, "Spare me a penny, kind sir."

"Here's a penny and welcome," said the soldier. "But it's all I can spare, for I've only six pennies left in the world."

"Where are you going then?" asked the old woman.

"I hardly know myself," said the soldier. "I suppose I must go to the city and beg my bread. That's what happens to old soldiers." But seeing the old woman look sad, he went on, "Don't worry about me, grandmother. Perhaps I shall have a stroke of luck. Suppose I find out how the princesses wear out their shoes? Then I'll become king and have a wife into the bargain."

"That's not so difficult," said the old woman unexpectedly. "Only you must be sure not to drink the wine they offer you when you go to bed. Pretend to drink it and then pretend to fall asleep. Here, take this cloak." And she took a short, shabby cloak out of her bundle and handed it to him. "It doesn't look much," she said. "But it will make you invisible. You can follow the princesses and find out where they go."

The soldier thought the old woman must be quite mad, but he didn't want to hurt her feelings, so he thanked her politely and took the cloak. He went towards the city, but after an hour or so the wind sprang up and he started shivering. "May as well put the cloak to some use," he said, "shabby as it is." He put it round his shoulders and stopped dead. He could no longer see himself.

"Merciful Heavens," he said. "It's true." He took off the cloak again, wrapped it up carefully in his bundle, and went on towards the city.

"The old woman must have been a witch," he thought. "Or a good fairy. Perhaps I could really find out where the princesses go to dance."

So he went to the palace, and though he was so poor and shabby he was made as welcome as any prince. When night fell he was led to the bed-chamber opening off the room where the princesses slept. They greeted him as politely as the other suitors and the eldest princess brought him a glass of wine. She smiled as she offered it to him, and he thought how beautiful she was, but he remembered what the old woman had said. He pretended to drink the wine but really he let it run down under his chin (and very sticky it felt). Then he lay down on the bed and pretended to snore.

The princesses laughed when they heard him, and then they took out their splendid gowns and dressed themselves for a ball. They were all in the highest spirits, except the youngest. "I don't know why it is," she said, "I feel so worried and miserable. I'm sure some terrible misfortune is going to happen."

"Don't be foolish, my darling," said the eldest princess. "Why are you always so timid? Remember how many princes have tried to guess our secret. This soldier, poor man, will be only too thankful for the chance of a good meal and a good sleep. He won't bother us."

All the same, she came to the open door between the two rooms and looked at the soldier, who kept his eyes shut and snored harder than ever. The princess seemed satisfied, and she went back to her bed and tapped it. At once it sank down through the floor, and a trapdoor appeared where the bed had stood. The eldest princess opened it and led the way down a long staircase into the darkness. The princesses followed her in turn, and the soldier sprang up, put on his cloak, and followed them. Because he was lame he found the stairs awkward, and once he stumbled and trod on the dress of the youngest princess, who was at the end of the line. She screamed and the line stopped.

They came to another forest where the trees were of gold and then to a third where they were made of diamonds. In each forest the soldier broke off a twig and each time the tree gave a crack and the youngest princess cried out in alarm. But the eldest repeated, "Our princes are firing salutes to welcome us."

As they came to the end of the diamond forest the soldier saw a lake and twelve little boats moored at the edge. In each boat sat a handsome prince and the princesses joined them, one to each boat. The soldier was still just behind the youngest princess, so he got in with her. The prince rowed away, but after a little while he said, "I can't think why the boat seems so heavy tonight."

"Everything is wrong tonight," said the youngest princess. "I feel so strange."

On the other side of the lake stood a splendid castle. Lights were blazing in every room, and drums and trumpets sounded a fanfare as the princes rowed their boats to the shore. They led the princesses into the castle's splendid ballroom, and there they danced and danced. The soldier amused himself by sometimes joining in the dance and giving one or other of the princesses an unexpected twirl, but they were too excited to notice, except for the youngest princess, who looked very upset whenever it happened to her. Once she left the dance and picked up a cup of wine, but the soldier took it out of her hand and drank it off. The princess looked terrified, but her eldest sister came up and scolded her gently. "Don't be foolish, my darling. You imagined it."

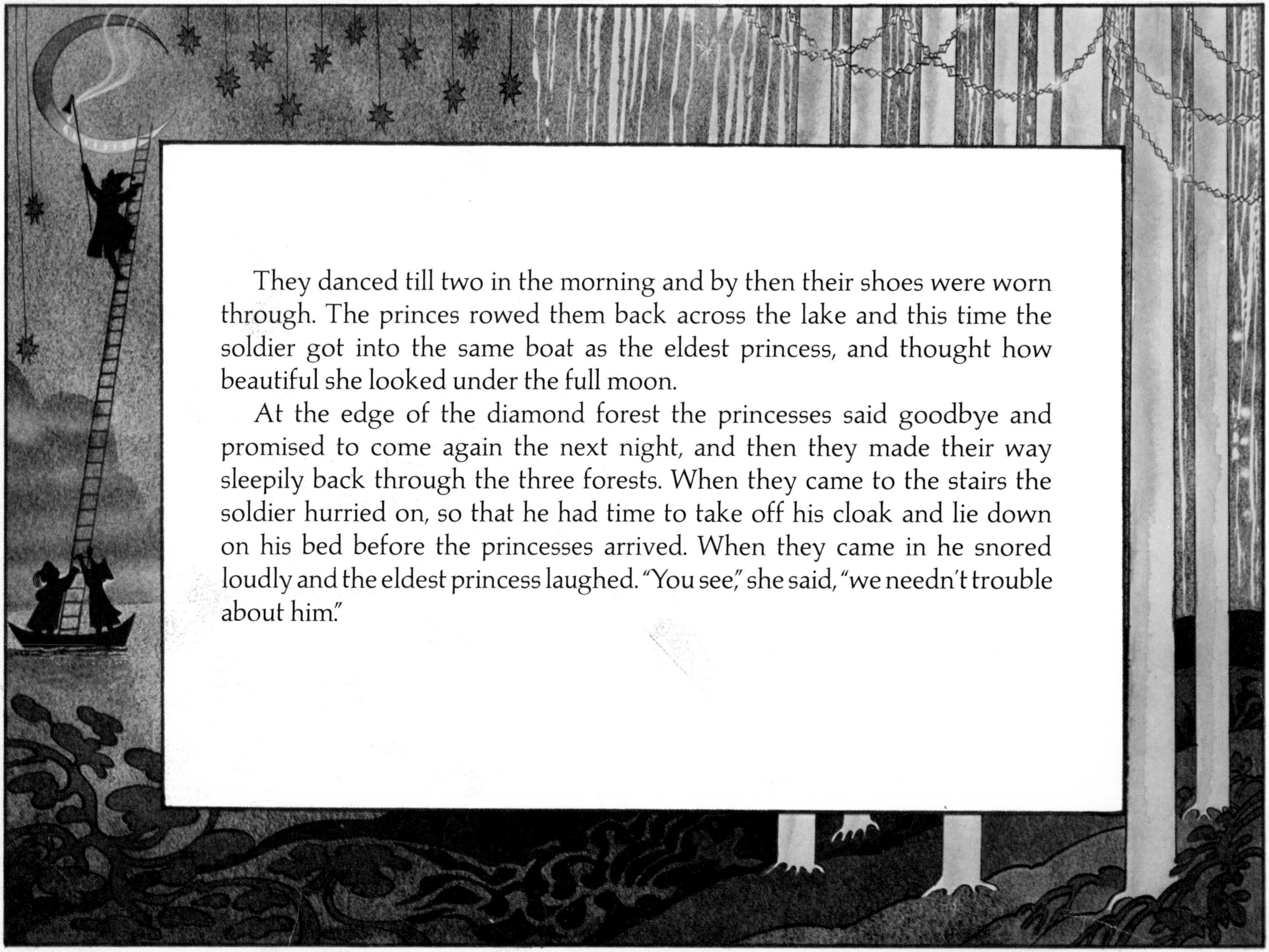

They danced till two in the morning and by then their shoes were worn through. The princes rowed them back across the lake and this time the soldier got into the same boat as the eldest princess, and thought how beautiful she looked under the full moon.

At the edge of the diamond forest the princesses said goodbye and promised to come again the next night, and then they made their way sleepily back through the three forests. When they came to the stairs the soldier hurried on, so that he had time to take off his cloak and lie down on his bed before the princesses arrived. When they came in he snored loudly and the eldest princess laughed. "You see," she said, "we needn't trouble about him."

Then they put their worn-out shoes in a row and went to bed. Next day the soldier said nothing, for he wanted to see the forests and the castle and the dancing again and sit beside the eldest princess as they crossed the lake. That night and again the night after he followed the princesses and everything happened as before except that he did nothing to frighten the youngest princess, though she still looked anxious. The third evening the soldier took one of the jewelled cups from the castle and put it in his pocket, to be an extra proof of his story.

The next morning the king sent for him. "You have spent three days with us," he said. "Now I must ask you: where do my daughters dance at night?"

"Sire," said the soldier, "they dance with twelve princes in a castle underground."

He heard a rustle of skirts behind a curtain and he guessed that the princesses were listening.

"How can that be?" said the king.

Then the soldier described the trapdoor and the three forests and the lake and the castle.

"This is a very strange story," said the king. "Can you prove it?"

For answer the soldier took from his pocket the silver twig and the golden twig and the diamond twig and the jewelled cup.

The king looked at them for a long time and then he said, "Come here, my daughters." They came out from behind the curtain and stood in a row. They all hung their heads, except for the eldest princess, who looked thoughtfully at the soldier.

"Is this true?" said the king to the youngest princess, who burst into tears. Then he asked each of his daughters the same question and none of them answered until he came to the eldest princess.

She laughed and said, "The soldier has been too clever for us. Yes, Father, it is all true."

"He has been too clever for you," said the king, "and now he can marry whichever of you he chooses."

The soldier looked at the row of princesses. The youngest one was still crying and her ten sisters looked indignant. But the eldest princess still looked thoughtful.

"I'm not as young as I was," said the soldier, "so I'll take the eldest."

At that the eldest princess burst out laughing. "There's a flattering reason," she said.

"It's a good reason," said the soldier. "You are the eldest and the cleverest and the most beautiful, and I've wanted to marry you ever since you gave me that sleeping draught."

"I believe a witch helped you," said the eldest princess.

"Or a good fairy," said the soldier.

The wedding was celebrated the same day with great splendour, the eleven younger princesses were bridesmaids, and the soldier and the eldest princess lived happily together all their lives.